The Field

The Field
Gary O'Connor

Edited by Jeremy Akerman and Eileen Daly

I am dancing. I have lights beneath my eyes and music in my head. I am spinning and falling. When I open my eyes I'm lying on my back looking up at a grey cloudless sky. I feel spots of rain on my face but they are so gentle it's hardly noticeable; in fact I question whether it is happening at all. I sit up. I am in the field.

My throat is dry and I can't remember the song. I think about this, I search my mind for the lyrics but they are gone. This doesn't bother me, sometimes I do forget. The last time I was here I sang *Sympathy for the Devil*. I like that one.

I get to my feet and look around. The landscape is so flat and featureless I always have trouble getting my bearings. I begin to walk. I'm not sure where I'm going, I just trust my instincts.

This all began with her. When I told her about the field she just laughed so I never mentioned it again. I remember picking up the telephone and hesitating, and Trish encouraging me.

She said, 'It's something you've always wanted to do so why not go for it. It will be fun.'

I dialled the number. It was an answer machine. It was her voice: 'Hi, you have reached Cath Sims. Sorry I can't take your call right now but please leave a message and I will get back to you.' She reminded me of someone else. I didn't leave a message, but I phoned back again just to listen to her voice. It sounded smoky, like a small dimly lit room in the back of my mind thick with cigarette smoke, something I can't usually tolerate, but in my head it neither irritated my eyes nor my breathing. It smelt like perfume, like the rich moist aroma of pipe tobacco before it is burnt.

I left a message this time, I gave my name and number and said that I was interested in having some singing lessons. Two days later Cath called me back. She wanted to know about me: had I sung before, what sort of songs I'd like to sing and what I was hoping to get out of the lessons. Cath recommended that I attend a minimum of six classes, and at 3pm the following Thursday I found myself outside St Matthew's church hall in Cambridge.

I parked my car at the front of the building and tried the main entrance. The door was locked. I circled the building and came across two other entrances but both also appeared to be locked. I wasn't able to see in through the windows and I couldn't hear any noise from inside. At the back of the church was a children's nursery, I could hear them playing. It felt awkward lurking around the doorway and I was about to give up when a rather short middle-aged woman appeared and asked me if I needed any help. I explained why I was there and she kindly invited me in. She said you could get to the hall via the nursery, and I followed her closely as she briskly navigated her way through a sea of toddlers and then through a small kitchen, to finally arrive at a rather Gothic-looking door. At this point she turned to me and smiled, then quickly disappeared back the way we had come.

I paused for a moment. I cannot remember why or what was going through my mind but I remember the silence. I could no longer hear the children playing, or the traffic outside the building. It was as if everything had stopped except me. I could hear my heart beating. I could feel tightness across my temples and the thud of blood moving around inside my head. The door handle looked like a knocker. I took the large iron ring in my hand and turned it to the left. When I opened the door it was as if a seal had been broken: a sudden surge of cold air hit me, immediately followed by the smell of old books and dying flowers, and the sound of children laughing and someone playing a piano.

As I opened the door wider I could see a woman standing in front of a piano with her back to me. She was tall. Her hair was tied back in a ponytail. I could see it had been dyed a shocking red colour but was now faded and grown out. Red cowboy boots, black leggings and a bright green bomber jacket completed the picture. She turned and smiled.

'Hello, you must be Daniel.'

Cath had a smile that took up most of her face. Her eyes were searching, calculating – adding me up, making rapid decisions about my character. In the few steps that it took to walk across the hall and shake her by the hand she needed to know me. I guess we all do it; I did it too.

I was very nervous but also excited. She put me at ease. We talked for a long time, too long in fact, I only had an hour and was eager to get started. Cath wanted to hear me sing and had asked me to bring a CD of songs to sing along to. This was harder than I thought: I have a large diverse collection of music and it's funny, but when I think about all of the songs I like, or even just a few, I'm confident I know all of the words but of course there are always one or two I get wrong or just can't remember. I wanted a song that I felt comfortable with, one that was uplifting and made me feel great. I chose *Another Girl Another Planet* by The Only Ones. I'd recently heard a debate on the radio about the way music affects us physically and emotionally. There's evidence that music excites receptors in the brain that in turn release chemicals that give us feelings of pleasure and euphoria, in much the same way as taking opiates do. Ironic then that this song has such a profound effect on me and yet contrary to common belief, the song is about taking heroin and not a love affair. In the conventional sense anyway.

I handed over the CD and Cath said, 'Fantastic – I haven't heard this in years.' She seemed genuinely excited. She put the disc into the CD player. She said we should start with some exercises.

The church hall was large and empty apart from the piano, a couple of tables and a few chairs stacked at the back next to the toilet. The hall looked Victorian: a large red brick shell clad on the inside with wooden panelling painted baby blue and broad wooden floorboards. Above our heads the rafters and beams were exposed. Acoustically it was not the best of spaces, every footstep and every word reverberated around us. Cath asked me to stand in the centre of the room with my feet apart and my toes pointing squarely forward. Standing in front of me she said, 'Bend your knees a little, straighten your back, bring your shoulders back and let your arms relax. Keep your chin up, but not too far, keep your head level and look straight ahead.' She asked me to relax but I could not relax in that position. She felt my shoulders and the small of my back. She held my forearms and looked into my eyes. I couldn't help laughing and she laughed too. 'I want you to put both of your hands on your tummy,' she said demonstrating this with a grin. I placed my hands low across my abdomen. I took a slow breath in through my nose and held it there for a moment then gently exhaled through my mouth. She then explained that when I exhale I should contract my abdominal muscles as if I were squeezing the air out of my body, and then relax them when I inhale. I could feel the muscles working beneath my palms. This was strange at first because I was doing the opposite to what I would naturally do. We did this several times and then moved on to making shushing sounds, as if telling a child to be quiet. I had to keep this sound going until I had no more breath left to exhale, then sharply inhale and start again. I found it hard to relax when inhaling, and the more that I thought about it the more difficult it became. Cath told me I had to be in touch with my body. I had to learn to use the lower part of my body to control and push the sound out. She said that it would not be long before singing in this way would feel natural to me and I would not need to think about it.

I get to the footpath that leads to the drain. I pull my collar up and look back at the field. The gun-metal sky pushes down hard on the land. The sky out here is so big. When I first came here I found all of this space difficult to deal with. I felt agoraphobic, fearful of being lost and forgotten. But once I had faced my fears I soon fell in love with the Fens. This place is bewitching; it will steal your heart without warning. I climb up the steep bank and walk along the edge of the drain. Like a canal it is long and straight. A light sprinkling of rain disrupts its surface and I can see a shoal of small fish in the water, they appear so expectant, as if waiting to be fed.

I was getting on well with Cath and there was no pressure to get things right. I was enjoying the experience but I hadn't actually sung anything up until that point. I was beginning to feel nervous, I was putting pressure on myself and I could feel it building. Singing is something I do in private: in the shower or when listening to music in the car. To sing in front of someone else is like stripping off naked and running through the centre of town. Vulnerable is an understatement. My time had come. This was why I was there, to cross the bridge – to jump the hurdles, to become a singer.

Cath said, 'Ok, let's try something. I just want to hear what you can do so I know what I've got to work with.' She gave me a wry smile. She could sense that it was going to be hard for me. She told me to relax, to take my time. Then she pressed play. I hadn't considered the lengthy guitar intro and waiting for the vocalist to come in seemed to take forever. I really did feel naked, standing there with someone I had only just met, not knowing whether I should wave my arms in the air, tap my feet or shake my arse. I wanted to show emotion but I felt so rigid, so stiff with anxiety and fear: would I remember the lyrics? Would I remember where to come in? How long would it go on for? The music moved around me like a ghost, and then finally, the unmistakable dry languid vocals of Pete Perrett came in. One of the most beautiful edgy pop songs ever written. I struggled to keep up. It should have made the charts – it should have been number one, but of course I was wrong about popular belief, it was obvious the song was about taking heroin and that's why it didn't get airplay. It was not a comfortable experience. I tried my best to engage with the song, to be passionate and absorbed in the performance but my mind kept straying: did Cath know that the song was about taking drugs? Does she think that I take drugs? Does she take drugs? Cath occupied the far end of the hall, rhythmically pacing from one side to the other, mouthing the words and watching me with interest.

I open my eyes.

I'm humming a tune.

I get to my feet and start walking in the direction of the drain.

Satisfaction by Devo – now that's a great cover. An excellent example in my humble opinion of how a band can deconstruct someone else's song and then reconstruct it and perform it in a startling new way. I was still battling with The Only Ones and trying to find my own way of doing it. My second appointment with Cath was at the same time on the following week. She told me that the double doors at the side of the building would be unlocked. I let myself in and Cath greeted me cheerfully. She had only just arrived herself. She looked different: she wore bright yellow shoes that were flat like little slippers and tight navy blue tracksuit bottoms that had two white stripes running down the outside of each leg with a little flair at the ankle. Her hair was worn down and it seemed darker than the week before. She had on a green top, it looked like it was made of silk, and had a low neckline trimmed with white lace. Over this she wore a black mohair cardigan with a small heart-shaped brooch pinned to it just above her right breast, its tiny stones caught the light as she moved. I liked the way she mismatched her clothing, nothing seemed to go together but it did, if you see what I mean. I was beginning to feel more confident with my singing. I had been practising in the car on the way into town but I was far from perfect. No matter how many times I sang along with the CD I would still slip up in one or two places. I swear my memory is getting worse.

We started the lesson with the warm-up exercises and as we progressed Cath introduced new ones. She would move around me then pause, looking thoughtful, then interrupt me saying, 'I think we should try this,' or 'You need to loosen up more, why don't we try...' Cath was tailoring the exercises to my needs, and it felt like I was growing in some way. Towards the end of the lesson we talked about our likes and dislikes in music. I was surprised to learn she sang in a soul band. She had the voice for it all right but there was something about her, her appearance, the way she carried herself. The way she looked at me. I visualised Cath in a cathedral filling its halls with haunting mantras sung in tongues or chanting rhythmic spells in the dead of night at a pagan gathering, or screeching melodic abuse at an audience of lost souls in some sweaty punk rock cellar bar. She was beginning to unwind me. She was beginning to take me apart. With each word, with each look, with each smile, she cut deeper. I was losing track of what was happening but I left that afternoon feeling energised. I fumbled through the glove compartment in my car looking for a new song to work on for the next lesson. I found what I was looking for. I started the engine and slid the disc into the CD player. As I took a left onto Long Road, an explosion of energy erupted inside the car. What an opening, what a song, what a singer...

I am standing at the centre of a large space. Around me from out of the shadows rise giant ivory columns. As I watch they appear to shift ever so slightly from one position to another. I can smell something sweet and warm in the air, it reminds me of cinnamon pastries. I look up and see a beautiful dome above my head. The structure is gilded in gold and decorated with images of naked men and women. Entangled, they twist and turn in a lustful orgy of colour. Now and then they become one forming a great serpent, the coils of its body fill the void of the dome. Hypnotically it slithers this way and that like an enormous reptilian kaleidoscope.

I can hear music. Someone is singing.

I don't want to move today. I feel very tired. I finger the soil as dark shadows come and go above my eyelids. Eventually I move up onto one elbow and look around me. I'm somewhere new, I'm still in the field – well at least I think I am. There is a footpath about eight or so metres off to my left. It winds its way along the edge of the field towards the remains of a small building. I get to my feet and walk towards it. There is a sharp wind coming at me from the east but it's a beautiful morning; a clear crisp start to the day. As I approach I can see that the building is, or should I say was, a cottage. There is no front door, the two windows either side of the entrance had been boarded up long ago but the wood has perished and some of it is missing. The roof has collapsed along with most of the first floor, filling the lower level with debris. I look in through the first window. I can see a small fireplace and some broken furniture. I go in through the doorway taking care not to disturb anything that may cause more of the floor above to collapse. It smells damp and mouldy, it reminds me of my grandmother's house. She cleaned her kitchen floor with a disgusting old mop. She never washed it or cleaned the water bucket out, it stank but she just kept on using it. Her sense of smell had long gone and her eyesight was bad too. She thought she was doing a good job. I pick up a chair from amongst the plaster and splintered wood. One of the legs is missing. I prop it up against a wall and look at it. Weeds and nettles have muscled their way up between the flagstones and rubble and there is an abundance of pigeon shit from where the birds have been nesting in what little there is left of the roof. I want to sit on the chair but I think it will break. I wonder who owns this place? It would be nice to do something with it. I push out some of the wood from one of the windows and look out at the view. Beyond the footpath is the field, and nothing more except two large white clouds resting on the horizon. 'It's beautiful,' I whisper to myself. Tomorrow I will bring something to mend the chair and maybe a broom to sweep the floor.

Music comes up between the floorboards. It seeps in through the walls, under the door and around the window frames. I can see the colours: swirls of pink, green, blue and purple moving around the room but all I can hear is the traffic outside on the street and someone turning a key in a lock in the hallway outside my door, and footsteps on the ceiling as the people in the flat above settle down for the evening.

It is raining. It's on days like this that I wish it would end. I look over my shoulder at the billowing blackness and I shudder. I head for the cottage. I push open the makeshift door and go to the only sheltered area at the far end of the building. I'd put polythene up earlier in the week. I sit beneath it on the chair and watch the raindrops map out tiny systems across the plastic sheeting. They dribble this way and that but go nowhere in particular. By the third lesson I felt I had reached a plateau. Don't get me wrong, I was still very much enjoying them but I felt that I wasn't progressing vocally. I had no intention of stopping, in fact I found my weekly meetings with Cath quite addictive and six just didn't seem to be enough. It was cold that afternoon. I'd arrived to find Cath dancing around the hall. I stood in the doorway and watched her. She looked as if she was dressed for the Antarctic. She had a white parka coat on, trimmed with fur; it was clearly several sizes too big for her. A knitted pink scarf was wrapped around her neck obscuring her nose and mouth and on her head was a blue ski hat and an enormous pair of headphones. I could hear the overspill of music coming from the headphones, it sounded distorted and tinny as she twirled around the space. I couldn't see her eyes beneath the dark sunglasses she was wearing and for the three or four minutes that I stood there I'm sure she didn't see me. Maybe Cath had been a dancer because she slid across the wooden floor with elegance and ease. Finally she stopped in front of me. She loosened the scarf revealing a big smile then took off the headphones and her hat.

'Do you like Alice Cooper,' she said, rosy-cheeked and slightly out of breath. I replied to her question with a nod as I watched her remove the coat and scarf. She kept the sunglasses on. I told her I had a new song to work on and she said great, it's good to try out different styles of singing to see how far I could push my voice.

She was right I needed to move on to something new – a new challenge to take me beyond the sense of apathy I was beginning to feel. We warmed up then I put on *Bankrobber* by The Clash; an easy song to remember but you really have to belt out those lyrics. Cath stood down the far end of the hall and told me to imagine throwing the words at her, as hard as I could. It was great, I was exhausted by the end of the session and felt back on track again.

Driving home my concentration drifted and I had to swerve hard to avoid hitting an oncoming car. It shook me up so much that I had to pull over into the nearest lay-by. I just sat there staring out of the window. I'm not sure for how long. I thought about the fragility of things, how everything in life is linked in some way from tiny microscopic organisms to the huge infrastructure of big cities and beyond. I thought about my parents and about my wife and our two sons, and about the few centimetres of separation between life and death. I felt so deflated, so empty, so alone. I had seen my own end hurtling towards me. I had survived and now I had to pay the price. The payment felt painful like a steel band encompassing my head. Numerous questions with nowhere to go were piling up inside my brain and the band was getting tighter and tighter. The big questions like what if and why and how pushed me into a corner – pushed me into a place where God will exist if I let him. I wanted him to be there, I wanted him to take my hand and comfort me but what if and why and how got there before him. Eventually I felt calm enough to drive again. It was only when I turned the key in the ignition that I realised I was looking out over a newly ploughed field. I remember thinking how beautiful it looked, like a field of dark chocolate.

Cath took off the motorcycle helmet and her raven black hair stuck to her forehead and cheeks, framing her unnaturally pale complexion. She looked unwell but it was a good look…I liked it. Her lips were blood red and made her mouth seem even bigger than usual. She took a crumpled white paper bag out of her pocket.

'Do you want one,' she said, offering it to me. 'They're aniseed twists, good for the voice – Harry Secombe swears by them.'

'Isn't he dead?' I asked her as I took one from the bag.

'Is he?' She looked concerned. 'When did that happen?'

'A long time ago,' I replied. 'Thanks, I haven't had one of these since I was a kid.'

There was that smile again. So ambiguous, so misleading. Cath put the bag of sweets back into her cardigan pocket and went over to the CD player and turned it on, she then turned to me and took both my hands and led me into the centre of the hall. I was smiling too; I wasn't sure what she was doing, maybe she wanted to dance? The music started and she let go of my hands and stepped back from me. It took me a moment to recognise the song. Cath began to move around me clawing at the air like some kind of wild animal. All I could do was grin. I felt awkward; it was both amusing and strange. Then suddenly Cath began shrieking. It was musical in a primitive sense. She began to laugh and encouraged me to join in, she was like a small child shouting and hollering for the pure enjoyment of it, making as much noise as possible, letting the world know it exists. She was letting go of herself, shaking off her inhibitions, and I joined her.

I stand on the small bridge looking down into the water. It's clear enough to see the bottom but it has an unusual red tint to it, as if the drain is full of rusting iron. I think it's just the result of rotting vegetation. I can feel her hands on my shoulders. Her long thin fingers work their way down my spine, her nails pierce my shirt and graze my skin; it takes my breath away. I look around but there is no one behind me.

I'd arrived to find Cath sitting at the piano, playing a piece of music I did not recognise. It was beautiful: delicate cascading notes fell from her fingertips and reverberated around the hall. I didn't want to disturb her so I approached quietly, but as soon as I came into view she stopped playing.

'That's wonderful,' I said, 'what's it called?

'It hasn't got a name,' she replied with a sniffle, then took a tissue out of her coat pocket and blew her nose. 'Sorry, I seem to have developed a cold.'

Cath's eyes were wet and puffy. She looked as if she had been crying. I didn't know what to say so I just smiled.

A murder of crows, now I've always thought that to be a fitting term when you think about the sinister connotations associated with those birds. I remember driving home from my parents' house one afternoon. I was approaching a T-junction at which I had to turn right. Ahead of me, through a hedge of hawthorn, I could see several crows standing on the roof of an abandoned car, which looked like it was from the 1950s, not that there was much left of it, just a rusting shell. There was no other traffic on the road so I paused for a moment to watch. The birds stood in a circle as if regarding one another. The largest of them hopped forward. It had a silvery grey hood similar to a jackdaw, but jackdaws are much smaller. This one appeared old and distinguished and strutted about cawing loudly. As I drove away, I couldn't help thinking they were planning some terrible deed.

Cath soon perked up and was back to her usual cheerful self. At the end of the lesson we sat for a while and talked. She told me about her home, a house that she'd inherited after her father's death.

'I'm not sure I could move from one place to the next like some people do,' she said. 'The house is very important to me.'

Cath was looking a little agitated.

'Was it your childhood home?' I asked. There was a moment's pause as if she had to think carefully about the answer, and then she nodded.

'It's the same for me,' I smiled, 'my mother still lives in the house where I grew up. I go to see her at least once a week and it always stirs up memories for me, but I don't have a strong connection with the place. In fact I was there last week and I was upstairs having just come out of the bathroom and I remember standing on the landing looking into my old bedroom, wishing for some kind of emotional response. I do think that objects and places have a resonance, an emotional, spiritual quality that develops through years of human contact. People can sense these things, but I felt so disappointed because I couldn't feel anything at all.

It was as if the house was made of cardboard.'

Cath laughed. 'Would you like to come around to my house?' Her words took me by surprise.

'Yes…yeh that would be nice.'

Now every time I see crows, pecking at road kill or combing fields looking for insects, the way they do, I know they're one step ahead of the game. There's more to them than meets the eye…they know far more than they let on.

My head is fucking killing me. I get to my feet. It's so misty I can't make out where I am.

'God it's cold.'

I pull my jacket tight across my chest. I'm shivering – I need to get off the field as quickly as possible. I start walking; the soil sticks to my shoes making my feet feel so heavy.

'What was that song?'

The lyrics are there somewhere, somewhere at the back of my mind – I can smell them, I can taste them, I can't feel my fingers anymore. 'Something about a boy being all alone, and needing someone.'

The cottage must be here somewhere. I change direction.

'On a rollercoaster, a funfair…looking for love.'

I'm so tired now. I can't feel my toes, I'm going to have to stop soon. His heart is broken, she loves another, she can't feel my fingers anymore.

It was a nice house, a small Victorian terrace on Shipton Street. Cath answered the door and invited me in. She was wearing a boiler suit and a Russian military hat that looked as if it was made from real bearskin. Cath showed me into the living room and we sat down in front of the fire.

'It's a lovely place,' I said, looking around the room in wonder.

'Thank you, would you like some tea or coffee?'

'Tea please.'

Cath got to her feet and went through to the kitchen. The walls were peppered with pictures: photographs, paintings and drawings of all sizes. There was a large antique dresser in one corner full of small porcelain figures and toy cars, and lots of books…books everywhere: on tables, shelves, in piles on the floor. Cath came back into the room holding a tray.

'Do you take sugar?'

I said no and took the teacup from her and sat back in my chair. There was an awkward silence as we sipped our tea in front of the roaring fire. Yet she kept that enormous hat on. She must have been so hot.

'Was your father an artist?' I gestured towards a wall of images with a chocolate digestive.

'No, not really, he just liked collecting things.' Cath leaned forward, 'He did like drawing, he always took a sketchbook and a box of charcoal with him whenever we went on holiday.' She took a sip of tea and smiled at me. 'He liked to sketch interesting buildings, old churches, that sort of thing. Being a child I found it all quite dull. His fingers were always black from handling the charcoal, he used to tweak my nose and pinch my cheeks and leave sooty grey marks all over my face.'

I looked at Cath's hands, at the way her long thin fingers cradled the teacup.

'I see you like to read.'

'Now and again,' Cath put her cup down. 'Most of these books belonged to my father and I've never read them, I just can't seem to let them go.'

I picked one up from the top of the nearest pile and wiped the dust from its cover with the back of my hand. 'This looks interesting,' I said as I flicked through the pages, stopping to read the title of each story I came across. As I put the book back a photograph fell from its pages. I picked it up, it was a black and white image of a young woman with her back to the camera, walking out across an open field. I turned it over; in the top right-hand corner, written in pencil, was the date 1952 and the letters JW. I looked across at Cath expecting a reaction but she showed no sign of interest. I looked at the picture again. It must have been very windy that day: the woman wore a long dark coat that clung to the back of her legs and her long fair hair was blown forward about her head; she was trying to hold it back from her face. I offered the photograph to Cath. She took it and said thank you.

'My father died of lung cancer six years ago.' Cath's eyes were fixed on mine, it was as if she was waiting for an answer rather than a sympathetic response. I had wondered how her father had died; in my mind I thought it might have been something more sensational like a plane crash or lost at sea, or even suicide. I'd wanted to ask her but couldn't bring myself to do it.

'He had been ill for a long time,' she said. 'It was a relief when it was all over.'

'I'm sorry to hear that,' I sat forward, sensing the tension in her voice and the inadequacy of my response. 'Do you have any brothers or sisters?'

'No, just me.'

'What about your mother?' I asked.

'She walked out years ago.'

'It must have been hard,' I said, 'dealing with it, all on your own.' Cath scrunched her face up like a child who had just tasted something it dislikes.

'Yes I suppose so, but I didn't think about it at the time. I just got on with it.' Cath took off her hat and sat back in the chair. 'That's better,' she said, running her fingers through her hair, 'I was beginning to cook under there! So, what are you going to do after the lessons? Are you going to join a band?'

'I don't know. It wasn't my intention. Learning to sing has always been on my to do list along with all the other madcap ideas. I've never thought of myself as an entertainer, but it's good to do something out of character, challenge yourself, broaden one's horizons.' Cath nodded in agreement. 'What about you?' I asked her, 'Do you have a list?'

'No, I just do things. But it's a good idea, I think I'll write one.'

I try the lighter again, it sparks this time. I try once more and a small blue flame licks the edge of the newspaper.

'Come on – come on!'

It smoulders then ignites. I place a few splinters of wood around the burning paper and gently nudge them into position hoping they'll take. The wind is fierce, it moans and whistles its way through the derelict building. The flames build and I add more wood. I rub my hands together above the heat and think about home. I miss Trish and the kids.

'Would you like some more tea?' Cath put the empty cups on the tray.

'No thank you. I should really be going.'

'Please stay, just for one more.' She seemed agitated, her eyes looked glazed and moist and just for a moment I thought she was going to cry.

'Ok,' I said and sat back in my chair. I watched her as she made her way back to the kitchen. I could hear a radio and the sound of her filling the kettle.

'Are you hungry?'

'Err...I could eat something,' I replied, as I made my way towards her.

'Would you like a sandwich? I have some ham.' Cath stood in front of an open fridge with a bread knife in her hand.

'Thanks, that would be nice.'

The kitchen was smaller than I expected. Or maybe it was big but just looked small because of all the junk in it. At the far end was a large ginger tom curled up on a table next to a bowl of fruit. I sat down and gave the cat a stroke behind its ear.

'Tell me about your family.' Cath put the tea and the sandwich in front of me.

'My wife's name is Trish and we have two boys, William and James.' Cath looked at me over the rim of her teacup. 'Will is nearly five and James is seven.'

'They must be quite a handful.'

'Yes, two boys bouncing around the house can be hard work.'

'Tell me about Trish.'

'She's perfect,' I answered, focusing on Cath's eyes. 'She's younger than me but so much wiser. It was her who encouraged me to take the singing lessons. Do you have...?' I fumbled for words; I was going to say partner or boyfriend but neither of those terms seemed to apply to Cath. 'I mean, is there someone special in your life?'

'No, I can't be doing with all that nonsense.' Cath looked away and just for a moment I thought she was being serious.

'Can I use the bathroom?' I asked.

'Sure, it's at the top of the stairs, on your right.'

I made my way to the front of the house and turned to climb the staircase. I had my foot on the first step when I looked up and saw an elderly man standing at the top looking down at me. I froze – I wasn't sure what to do next. As I looked at him the face of a young girl peered out from behind his legs, the child clung to the man like a scared animal. I stepped back in surprise and just for a second looked away. When I looked up again they had gone.

'Daniel.'

'Err…yes.'

'Are you Ok?' Cath placed her hand on my forearm; her voice was soft and enquiring.

'Yes, yes I'm fine,' I finished my tea. 'Can I use the bathroom before I go?'

'Sure, it's at the top of the stairs, on your right.'

I pick up the black feather and run it through my fingers. The tiny globules of dew collect and trickle into the palm of my hand, I think of her. I put it into my pocket and go into the cottage. I have decided to move some of the rubble to the far end of the building to give myself more room. I pick up as much as I can carry and dump it among the nettles and brambles that dominate the exposed area. This is where the kitchen must have been: the remains of a ceramic sink lay beneath a frameless window and the rusted gears of a washing mangle protrude from the debris like a piece of modernist sculpture. I go back and pick up several bricks and some wood and add them to the pile. I wonder why this place was abandoned. I throw more wood to the floor. Suddenly I can see things I never noticed before, things that tell a story – that give clues to who had lived here: a broken teacup, a tobacco tin, a button. I push aside the nettles and weeds with my feet and prod the rubble with a stick.

I find an old penny; I spit on it and clean it on my jacket sleeve. It reveals the unmistakable silhouette of Queen Victoria. Her features had faded; countless exchanges between fingers and pockets have rendered the coin smooth and thin. I like the feel of it. I roll it between my fingers. I go over to the fireplace and place the penny on top of the mantelpiece along with the crow feather from my pocket. I pick up an armful of bricks and make my way over to the nettles. As they fall to the ground I notice something else, something small and shiny at my feet. I kneel down for a closer look and carefully ease the object from the soil. I make my way to the other end of the cottage where rainwater has collected in the folds of the polythene sheeting, I submerge my find and rinse it clean. I hold the brooch up to the light; its encrusted surface twinkles as it rotates in my fingers. A fine line of tiny red stones zigzag their way across the jewel splitting it in two.

'Come on! That's bloody dreadful you can do better than that,' Cath hit the piano key laughing. I tried the note again but I found it hard to be serious. She came up behind me, took me by the shoulders and gave me a gentle shake, 'Relax, relax,' she breathed into my ear, 'I could eat you whole.' I turned to face her but Cath was already walking away from me.

'Sorry…what did you say?'

'Relax!' She yelled jovially, 'Lets try the song again.'

Cath gave me a puzzling look, 'What are you thinking about?'

'Crows,' I muttered. 'I saw a dead one on the road this morning. It's not something you see very often, if you think about it.'

'Why's that?'

'They're clever birds…crows. Too clever to be hit by cars.'

'Not like pheasants then,' Cath sat cross-legged on the floor and offered me a sweet that resembled a small fried egg from the paper bag she was holding.

'No thanks.'

'I liked collecting feathers when I was a girl,' she said chewing on a sweet.

'We always thought it was good luck to find a crow's feather and bad luck if you picked up one from a magpie. Magpies are clever birds too you know. My father stuck some kind of silver foil over our bathroom window, it allowed us to look out, but from the outside it was like a mirror so no one could see in.'

'I know the stuff you mean,' I interrupted.

'There was this magpie that would turn up each morning and sit on our windowsill admiring itself, it pecked at the window pane and made all sorts of wonderful sounds. I could push my nose up against the glass and look into its eyes and it would never see me – it was amazing. I suppose that's not particularly clever, but it shows a certain amount of intelligence,' Cath grinned, bunching her skirt and bringing her knees up to her chin.

There is a fire beyond my eyelids, a warmth that makes my face tingle with pleasure, a warmth that fills my nostrils with ants and worms, with dew and broken grass, and the ammonia of fox piss and nettles. The sound of birds and insects fill the air. I roll over and look up through a sea of green at a blue cloudless sky. I can hear the lyrics in my mind. It's a good day for a song the voice tells me. I get to my feet and wade through the grass towards the footbridge. A light breeze ruffles the reeds at the edge of the water, sprigs of tiny yellow flowers fight for sunlight among the tall tufts of foliage that covers the field. I leave the bridge and follow the drain looking for insects and interesting pieces of flint as I go. Ahead of me I can see a large tree, its blackened shape stands at a bend in the field that sweeps around to my right and away from the drain; this new boundary is formed by a ditch crowned with brambles and blackberries. The air is suddenly still as I reach the tree. Nothing seems to be moving, not even a blade of grass. I look up at the branches, thin and lifeless, like bony fingers they reach out above my head. I know this place but I can't remember ever being here before. This thought makes me feel uncomfortable, like I'm being watched. I look over my shoulder expecting to see somebody there. I turn my attention back to the tree, it is hollow, a split down its middle exposes a deep dark chasm that emits a pungent smell of decay. Nothing grows beneath the tree: an arc of dried earth has claimed this corner of the field. I kneel down and pick up a handful of soil. I let it fall through my fingers as I watch the horizon.

The jazz tune on the radio sounds like it is being played through a tin can. I'm not really fond of jazz, the only piece I can name is *Take Five* but I couldn't tell you who wrote it, or who performed it. But I like listening to jazz on the radio, it makes me feel cultured and sophisticated. I pick up the radio and move it from the chair to the mantelpiece and adjust the tuning. The reception is still bad; I adjust the aerial but the sound is no better than before. I put more wood on the fire. It is getting late but there is a bright moon tonight and I can see quite well. I take my torch and go back to the kitchen. It's a balmy evening, and there is a wonderful floral scent in the air. I pick up the broom and continue sweeping. The cleared area has revealed a beautiful stone floor. I run the torchlight over it, admiring my work. I'm drawn to one flagstone, I'm not sure why. Gently I explore its surface with my fingers, it feels warm and nice. It's loose. I push against it and it pivots ever so slightly. I look around for some kind of tool to use, I find a rusty hinge and start scraping out the detritus from around the stone. I can just get the tips of my fingers underneath it but I can't quite lift it. Excitedly I scan the far end of the building with the torch, searching for something to use. I pull a length of wood from the nettles and hurry back to the stone. I wedge the wood underneath it and lever it free. Beneath the flagstone is a hole. I stop, I'm not sure why. I feel light-headed and nauseous, the scent in the air is intense, it smells sweet and sickly like lilies. Shapes in the shadows appear to be closing in on me, I shine the torch around me, this way and that, trying to reassure myself that everything is Ok. I dip the light into the hole. I see a bundle. I hesitate before reaching in and retrieving it. I go over to the fire and lay it on the floor. The fabric is heavily stained: it's dark and crusty to touch but in the firelight I can make out the print of tiny blue flowers. I carefully unfold the bundle and find a hammer. I grit my teeth, the metallic frequencies from the radio cut through my head like chalk across a blackboard – I grab the radio and throw it against the wall.

I run at the bank, up through the grass to the ridge and look down at the water stretching out along the edge of the field off into the distance. The surface is perfect, undisrupted like a sheet of glass. I begin walking. I follow the course of the drain towards the sun that sits low in the sky. I watch the water intently, looking for insects and other signs of life. A couple of goldfinches perform an aerial dogfight among the reeds before swooping off across the field; an emerald dragonfly appears at my side, it hovers in front of my face then falls back to the edge of the water. Soon it returns, circling me at close quarters, it doesn't stray any further than a metre or so before it's back again. I feel as if the creature is studying me. I hear a gloopy plop in the water behind me as a fish breaks the surface, I turn my head to catch a glimpse but all I see are ripples. Ahead of me I can see something in the water. As I approach I make out the wing of a large bird, the feathers fan out, rising up like slender fingers in a white glove. As I draw near my first thought is confirmed: a swan floats lifeless, drifting gently mid stream. I walk with the swan, looking on as its long neck slowly uncoils and dips deeper into the shadows, as its body slowly spins and rolls majestically in the fading light. Our pace is matched by the stillness of the afternoon, I breathe in deeply, wanting to absorb the moment. I have this strange euphoric sensation: I feel peaceful and relaxed but there's a raging sense of excitement deep down in my stomach, like tiny explosions. I feel it moving up into my chest. I can't think of anywhere else I would rather be right now than here. I watch her rise and fall. There isn't a mark on her body. I wonder how she came to be here.

As the sun goes down the water becomes darker, impenetrable to the eye; she looks even more beautiful, like freshly fallen snow. I walk with her as far as I can until she fades from view.

I've been looking at my hands for so long now that I've forgotten why I'm doing it. I know I should be doing something else, but I can't think what. There are blisters and cuts on my fingers; the skin is so dry it's beginning to split. I turn my hands over and pick at the dirt underneath my nails. Looking at them makes me feel old. I pull up my shirtsleeves; I'm sure I had a watch on my wrist, it was silver with a large black face. It had a brown leather strap that smelt bad because I never took it off when washing my hands. That reminds me, I should really change that strap. I take another book from the pile in front of me and run my fingers over the cover. It's a book of poetry. I like listening to poetry but I find it hard to read. What I mean is, the words feel less powerful in my head, I have trouble grasping the rhythm in which they were intended to be delivered. But I like listening to poets reading their work; it's not just about the words, it's also the voice of the person who conceived them, that's what makes them so powerful. I open the book and flick through the pages coming to rest somewhere in the middle. I press my face against the words and breathe in deeply. The complex scent has notes of musky oils, decaying flowers, the voice of a teacher I had as a boy and the weight of my youngest son asleep in my arms. The sweetness of things I just can't find the words to express, and the smell of fear and anticipation.

I breathe in again.

The stone is smooth; I turn it over in my hand as I head for the tree and place it with the others. Walking over to the edge of the field I pick up another stone, the largest I can find, then return to the tree. One by one I place the stones alongside each other and a semicircle begins to take shape. I stand up and step back to take a look. For some reason serpents in trees comes to mind. I pick up another stone and continue. I step back again. It looks like a serpent but then again it could be the letter S. I'm fine with both notions but the letter S is beginning to trouble me.

I wonder how old the tree is. It must have died long ago but it's still very beautiful. It lurches forward like an unsteady giant about to fall to the ground. I go over and place a hand against the bark, which feels cold and damp. I put my right foot against the tree, dig my fingers into the bark and pull myself up. It's not so difficult – there are plenty of nooks to get a footing and a number of good points to cling to, but I'm taking my time because it feels so slimy and I'm frightened of slipping. I reach the hole and pull myself up to the edge. It smells dank. Looking down into the darkness I think about her. I position myself safely and remove my boots. I tie the lace of the left one to a branch and let it drop; it swings vigorously before slowly rotating. I watch this for a moment then tie the second boot to another branch and let go. I smile. I take off my socks and drape them across two separate twigs then climb further up into the tree and take off my shirt and hang this too among the branches. Now I work my way over to the other side of the tree and take off my jeans. I throw them across an out-reaching branch and they sway momentarily before falling and coming to rest on a lower bough. I take off my underwear and place them as high up in the branches as I dare go. I climb back down to the edge of the cavity. I hold my breath and close my eyes. Carefully, I lower myself in.

It was raining as I pulled into the car park and I could see a man in a suit holding an umbrella, waiting at the front entrance. I slammed the car door behind me and hurried towards him, 'Mr Pepper?' I asked, offering him my hand, 'I'm Daniel.'

'How do you do,' he sniffed, 'terrible weather,' his wet hand slipped into mine. 'Shall we go in?' he said, fumbling with a large set of keys. I held his umbrella while he pushed open the heavy oak doors. Pepper stood to one side and with a smile, allowed me to go first. I stepped inside and slowly circled the space.

'What days do you have available?' I asked.

'Well, at the moment we can do Friday afternoons,' Pepper shook his umbrella in the doorway, 'or you could have it for the whole day on Wednesdays, but I suggest you let me know as soon as possible because the school holidays are coming up and we get very busy.'

I paused by the piano and listened to the rain as it fell in waves against the windows.

'Wednesdays are perfect,' I whispered.

The Field by Gary O'Connor
Edited by Jeremy Akerman
and Eileen Daly

Published in 2009 by
Transition Editions
Unit 25a
Regent Studios
8 Andrews Road
London E8 4QN

Transition Editions is the publishing
wing of Transition Gallery

The Field is Edition 006

ISBN 978-0-9548954-5-7

With thanks to Jeremy Akerman,
Eileen Daly, Cathy Lomax and
Arts Council England for their support.

LOTTERY FUNDED

A complete catalogue record for
this book can be obtained from the
British Library on request.

Designed by Untitled
Printed by Lancing Press